Inside a Barn in the Country

A Rebus Read-Along Story

by Alyssa Satin Capucilli
Illustrated by Tedd Arnold

Cartwheel
·B·O·O·K·S·®

SCHOLASTIC INC.
New York Toronto London Auckland Sydney

Library of Congress Cataloging-in-Publication Data

Capucilli, Alyssa.
Inside a barn in the country / by Alyssa Capucilli ; illustrated by Tedd Arnold.
p. cm.
Summary: One after another, the animals in a barn wake each other up
with the unique sounds they make.
ISBN 0-590-46999-1
[1. Domestic animals—Fiction. 2. Animal sounds—Fiction. 3. Stories in rhyme.]
I. Arnold, Tedd, ill. II. Title.
PZ8.3.C1935In 1995   92-30491
[E]—dc20 CIP AC

12 11 10 9 8 7 6 5 4 3 2 1   5 6 7 8 9/9 0/0

Printed in Singapore

First Scholastic printing, March 1995

For Peter and Laura with love
—A.S.C.

For Donavan and Beth
—T.A.

Here is a barn in the country.

Here is the mouse that squeaked
in the hay
inside a barn in the country.

Here is the that squeaked
in the hay

and woke up the horse that
whinnied *neigh*
inside a barn in the country.

Here is the 🐭 that squeaked
in the hay
and woke up the 🐴 that
whinnied *neigh*

that woke up the cow that
started to *moo*
inside a barn in the country.

Here is the that squeaked
in the hay
and woke up the that
whinnied *neigh*
that woke up the that
started to *moo*

that woke up the rooster
cock-a-doodle-doo
inside a barn in the country.

Here is the that squeaked
in the hay
and woke up the that
whinnied *neigh*
that woke up the that
started to *moo*
that woke up the
cock-a-doodle-doo

that woke up the chicks that
started to *peep*
inside a barn in the country.

Here is the 🐭 that squeaked
in the hay
and woke up the 🐴 that
whinnied *neigh*
that woke up the 🐄 that
started to *moo*
that woke up the 🐓
cock-a-doodle-doo
that woke up the 🐤🐤 that
started to *peep*

that woke up a couple of sleepy
white sheep
inside a barn in the country.

Here is the ![mouse] that squeaked
in the hay
and woke up the ![horse] that
whinnied *neigh*
that woke up the ![cow] that
started to *moo*
that woke up the ![rooster]
cock-a-doodle-doo
that woke up the ![chicks] that
started to *peep*
that woke up a couple of sleepy
white ![sheep]

that woke up the dog that
started to *bark*
inside a barn in the country.

Here is the 🐭 that squeaked
in the hay
and woke up the 🐴 that
whinnied *neigh*
that woke up the 🐄 that
started to *moo*
that woke up the 🐓
cock-a-doodle-doo
that woke up the 🐤🐤 that
started to *peep*
that woke up a couple of sleepy
white 🐑🐑
that woke up the 🐕 that
started to *bark*

that woke up the pig that snored
in the dark
inside a barn in the country.

Here is the 🐭 that squeaked
in the hay
and woke up the 🐴 that
whinnied *neigh*
that woke up the 🐄 that
started to *moo*
that woke up the 🐓
cock-a-doodle-doo
that woke up the 🐤 that
started to *peep*
that woke up a couple of sleepy
white 🐑
that woke up the 🐕 that
started to *bark*
that woke up the 🐖 that snored
in the dark

that woke up the hens that
started to *cluck*
inside a barn in the country.

Here is the 🐭 that squeaked
in the hay
and woke up the 🐴 that
whinnied *neigh*
that woke up the 🐄 that
started to *moo*
that woke up the 🐓
cock-a-doodle-doo
that woke up the 🐤🐤 that
started to *peep*
that woke up a couple of sleepy
white 🐑🐑🐑
that woke up the 🐕 that
started to *bark*
that woke up the 🐷🐷 that snored
in the dark
that woke up the 🐔🐔 that
started to *cluck*

that woke up a very loud
honking old duck
inside a barn in the country.

Here is the 🐭 that squeaked
in the hay
and woke up the 🐴 that
whinnied *neigh*
that woke up the 🐄 that
started to *moo*
that woke up the 🐓
cock-a-doodle-doo
that woke up the 🐤 that
started to *peep*
that woke up a couple of sleepy
white 🐑
that woke up the 🐕 that
started to *bark*
that woke up the 🐖 that snored
in the dark
that woke up the 🦆 that
started to *cluck*
that woke up a very loud
honking old 🪿

that woke up the farmer

who sat up and said,

inside a barn in the country.